marty mcguire

has too many pets!

marty mcguire

has too

many pets!

BY KATE MESSNER

ILLUSTRATED BY BRIAN FLOCA

SCHOLASTIC PRESS / NEW YORK

Library of Congress Cataloging-in-Publication Data

Messner, Kate.

Marty McGuire has too many pets! / by Kate Messner; illustrated by Brian Floca. — 1st ed.   p. cm.

Summary: After visiting a great ape sanctuary, Marty and her friends set out to raise the money to "adopt" a chimpanzee by organizing a talent show at school and starting a pet-sitting business in Marty's basement—which soon gets out of hand.

1. Pet sitting—Juvenile fiction. 2. Money-making projects for children —Juvenile fiction. 3. Animal sanctuaries—Juvenile fiction. [1. Pet sitting—Fiction. 2. Money-making projects—Fiction. 3. Animal sanctuaries—Fiction.] I. Floca, Brian, ill. II. Title.

PZ7.M5615Mf 2014   813.6—dc23

ISBN 978-0-545-53559-5

For the Ward kids —
Bethany, Jenna, Will, and Ivy
— K.M.

For my sister,
Elizabeth
— B.F.

chapter 1

"How long until we get there?"

"It's just down the road," Dad says, "and please stop kicking my seat."

"Sorry." I put my feet down and try to keep them still. I don't *mean* to be a seat kicker, but it's hard when you've been in the car for an hour and you are going to see real live chimpanzees. "I'm excited."

Annie smiles over at me. "I hope they're out when we get there," she says.

"They might not be." Mom looks at us over her shoulder. "Remember, the sanctuary isn't a zoo. If you don't see the chimps today, you may have a chance when you come back to pick me up next weekend."

My stomach gets a little achy when she says that. "I wish you weren't going to be gone so long."

"Don't worry, Marty," Dad says in the chipper voice he uses when he's trying to get me to do chores. "We're going to have a fan-tabulous week."

"I know." But my eyes get watery and I hate that, so I look out the window at the farms and fields whooshing past. Mom's never been gone this long, and even though it's the coolest thing ever that she got chosen to work with these chimps for a week, I'm going to miss her.

"I wish kids were allowed to volunteer," I say.

"I know, Marty," Mom says. "But these are retired lab chimpanzees. They were used for years in experiments while scientists were trying to learn about human diseases and find cures for them. Carol started this sanctuary so the chimps could have a better life now, and that's wonderful, but they're still wild animals. They're powerful and strong, and they can be dangerous. They've been through a lot. It's just not a place for kids."

"I'm glad we get to see it anyway," Annie says.

She changes the subject. "Have you decided what to do for the third-grade talent show?"

"Not really." I don't have indoor talents. Catching frogs and jumping over streams aren't the kinds of things you can do on a stage.

"Veronica Grace asked me to be in her group," Annie says.

"Hmph." Veronica Grace loves tiaras and fancy dresses and doesn't like frogs, worms, or me. "What's she doing? Some frilly-face princess fashion show?"

"Marty, that's not nice," Mom says from up front. I hate how moms are always listening even when they look like they're not.

"It's a dance thing," Annie says. "You should be in it, too."

Before I can tell her no, Dad slows down and says, "Is this where we go?"

Dad turns down a long driveway and pulls the van up to a big building with a fenced-in area on one side. Annie and I are practically hanging out the windows, looking for chimps. I have my camera all ready, but the only animal around is a boring dog by the doorway.

"Where *are* they?" I ask.

"Maybe inside having lunch," Mom says as she opens the van door to let us out. "Come on into the reception area, and you can meet Carol."

We go inside, and Carol is easy to find but she's nowhere near as exciting as a chimpanzee. She's a plain old grandma-looking lady wearing hiking boots, jeans, and a sweatshirt. "Welcome! We're so thankful to have you here this week." She gives Mom a big hug and smiles at Annie and me. "I see you've brought along some future volunteers."

"This is my daughter, Marty, and her friend Annie," Mom says. "They were hoping for a quick look at the chimps before they head home."

"It's nice to meet you." Carol shakes our hands. "Unfortunately, our chimps make their own schedules, and they're pretty well settled in for the afternoon. But . . ." She steps over to a window behind the big reception desk and peers out into a big open space. "Oh, good! Come on over, and you can see a couple in the courtyard."

She points to a big wooden climbing thing that looks a lot like our jungle gym at school. "See Rosco there?"

"Oh! I see him!" Annie jumps up and down a few times. I look and look and finally spot a big, furry blob sacked out on a platform of the jungle gym.

"Rosco looks like my dad after Thanksgiving dinner," I say.

Carol laughs. "Here comes Chloe to tease him."

I press my nose against the glass and watch a smaller chimp climb up onto the platform where

Rosco is snoozing. She pokes her finger in his ear, and he swats her hand away, and pretty soon they're wrestling like Jimmy Lawson and Alex Farley during recess.

Finally, Rosco gives up, climbs down, and goes inside. Chloe just sits there looking around, like she's wondering what happened to all the fun. I'm sad, too. I could have watched them play forever.

"Come on, girls," Dad says. "Mom has work to do, and we need to head home."

"I wish we could stay," I say. "I didn't even get to take a picture."

"I can solve that problem." Carol hands me a Great Ape Sanctuary brochure from the big desk. She gives Annie one, too. "You can take these home and read about all the chimps your mom will be working with."

Annie opens hers up to a page that says *SUPPORT THE GREAT APES*. "Hey! You can adopt a chimp?"

"Awesome!" I say.

"It's a program we have so people can support the chimps by providing them with food and toys," Carol says. She looks at me. "You don't actually get to take one home."

It's like she could read my mind or something. I was already figuring out where our chimp would sleep. "It's still neat," I say. "Can we adopt one, Dad?"

He looks at the brochure. "It's kind of expensive." He's right. Chimps must eat and play a lot. "But I bet you could save your allowance and figure something out. Let's talk on the way home."

chapter 2

I'm bad at good-byes, so I hug Mom super fast and get in the van, and then I'm glad we have those brochures. The whole way home, Annie and I make plans to adopt our chimp.

"We should adopt Chloe," Annie says, tapping Chloe's big, furry face on the page. "She's been there the longest."

"Or Skipper," I say. "He looks the saddest. We should adopt both of them!"

"Maybe you should figure out how to raise the money first," Dad says as we drive back into town.

"We could have a bake sale," Annie says.

"Mrs. Aloi probably won't let us do that right away. She's busy with the talent show." Our teacher loves projects, but she has these maracas that she shakes when she gets stressed and needs us to quiet down. She's been shaking them a lot lately. "Hey! Let's ask Mrs. Aloi if we can charge admission to the talent show."

"Great idea!" Annie says. "Maybe we can do a bake sale later."

All this bake-sale talk is making me hungry. "Are we stopping for food, Dad?"

"No. Grandma's staying with us while Mom's away because I have a busy week at school with parent-teacher conferences. She's taking care of dinner," Dad says.

"Woo-hoo!" I pump my fist in the air.

"Grandma Joyce," Dad adds.

"Oh." I put my fist down. When my mom's mom, Grandma Barb, takes care of dinner, it means pepperoni pizza from Tony's and Lemon-Lime-Fizzy-Whiz soda. But Grandma Joyce is my dad's mom, and she's the boring grandma, even

though I'm never supposed to tell her that. So dinner will probably be weird tuna casserole and mushy green beans.

When Dad turns onto our street, Grandma's big old green Cadillac is already in the driveway.

"Want to stay for dinner?" I ask Annie.

"No, thanks." She's had Grandma Joyce's tuna casserole before. She waves and runs across the yard to her house, and I follow Dad up to the porch.

As soon as he opens the door, a big old tuna cloud swallows us up.

"Hi, Mom." Dad walks to the stove to hug Grandma Joyce.

"Hi, Grandma." I give her a hug, too. "Annie and I are going to adopt a chimpanzee! Maybe two!"

Grandma Joyce stirs her carrots and peas and shakes her head. "It looks like you've already adopted some rodents. I found mouse droppings when I was cleaning out your cupboard under the sink this afternoon."

"Mice? Cool! Emma Lashway has a pet mouse. She taught it how to go through a cardboard maze she built."

Grandma looks at me as if we are not even from the same planet.

"Mom, why were you cleaning under our sink?" Dad asks.

"It was a mess," Grandma says. "I scrubbed the refrigerator, too."

"You're not going to clean my playroom in the basement, are you?" I ask. Things disappear when Grandma cleans.

"Trust me," Dad says, "you don't want to go down there. It's such a mess it's been declared a federal disaster area."

Grandma laughs. "You have my word I'll stay out of the basement," she says, "but the rest of this house is getting a good scrubbing. I'll need your help moving the living room furniture so I can vacuum tomorrow."

Dad groans.

I give him my best chipper voice. "Don't worry, Dad. We're going to have a fan-tabulous week."

chapter 3

When Dad drops me off at school on Monday, Rupert and Alex are hanging on the monkey bars, and Veronica Grace has taken over the rest of the playground with her dance.

"You have to shimmy your shoulders," Veronica Grace tells Emma. "Like this." Veronica Grace

shimmies her shoulders, only her shimmy is more of a twitchy-wiggle.

"It looks like you're trying to shake off bugs," I say as I walk past.

"Marty!" Veronica Grace stops shimmy-wiggling. "We need people for our talent show number. Annie says you're good at gymnastics."

"No, I'm not." I *can* do cartwheels, but I'm not going to do them wearing some fancy-pants Veronica Grace outfit. "Hey, you guys," I call to Rupert and Alex. "Want to help with our adopt-a-chimp fund-raiser?"

Rupert drops to the ground. "Sorry. I can't. My mom says if I bring home one more order form for cheap wrapping paper or cookie dough, she's going to march back to school and shove it up somebody's nose."

Rupert's mom runs marathons and is not the kind of person you want to mess with, so I don't push it. "What about you?" I ask Alex. "We think the talent show could be a great fund-raiser if we charge admission."

"Sure!" He lowers himself from the monkey bars and walks over to the bench to get his tool belt. He usually wears it everywhere, but he must have taken it off so tools wouldn't fall out when he was upside down. "Where are we gonna keep the chimp? Need me to build a cage?"

"We don't keep the chimp. We're just donating money."

Alex looks disappointed, but he says, "I'll help. And my talent show act is going to be the coolest thing ever."

"What are you doing?" I ask.

"Sawing."

"Sawing? That's . . . interesting."

"I know, right?" Alex's face lights up. "Most people have no idea how to saw a board in half properly. Mick Buzzsaw on *Handyman America* says it's a real art."

When we go inside, Mrs. Aloi's "Third-Grade Stars Today" list is written on the board. *TALENT SHOW ASSIGNMENTS* is in big huge letters right after the morning math lesson.

Annie and I tell Mrs. Aloi about how we want to raise money for the chimps. She says that's a great idea, and we'll talk about it after math. I'm excited, but I still have no idea what to do for a talent. I wish I played an instrument.

"Today," Mrs. Aloi says, "we're going to talk about fractions."

Maybe I could ride a unicycle. I could probably get Alex to bring his tools over and take one of the wheels off my bike.

Mrs. Aloi brings out a big plastic pizza on a plate. "If we have twelve slices in this pizza and I eat six of them, what have I eaten?" she asks.

Jimmy Lawson waves his hand.

"More than your share," he says when she calls on him. "My dad always does that. My mom calls him Pizza Pig."

Making pizza would be a cool talent, I think. I could toss the dough like those guys at Tony's. Only I don't know how to toss dough.

Grandma Barb tried to teach me to juggle with beanbags once, but I kept dropping them.

"Marty?" Mrs. Aloi says. "What fraction of the pizza have I eaten now?"

She's pulled three plastic pieces off the big round plate.

"Umm . . . a third?"

"Not quite. Rasheena?"

"One-fourth," Rasheena says, and that's the answer.

Fractions are obviously not my talent.

Finally, Mrs. Aloi says it's talent show time. She picks up her marker and puts everybody's name on the white board. "Our talent show is in one week. Today, you need to let me know what you're going to do. Who would like to go first?"

Veronica Grace waves her arm like crazy.

"Veronica Grace?"

"I'm going to lead a dance extravaganza."

"Great." Mrs. Aloi scribbles *DANCING* next to Veronica's name.

Veronica Grace frowns a little. "It's spelled D-A-N-C-E E-X-T-R —"

"I know how to spell 'extravaganza.'" Mrs. Aloi spells it out. "Who's in your group?"

"Isabel, Annie, Kimmy, Emma, and —"

"I'm not dancing," Emma says. "I want to play my recorder."

"But you practiced with us!" Veronica Grace's face gets all red.

Emma shrugs. "I want to play the 'Happy Birthday' song instead."

"Whose birthday is it?" Rupert looks around.

"Nobody's," Emma says. "But that's the only song I know."

Mrs. Aloi writes *"HAPPY BIRTHDAY"—RECORDER* by Emma's name. She writes *DANCE EXTRAVAGANZA* next to Isabel's and Annie's names and starts to add it by Kimmy's.

"Wait!" Kimmy says. "I don't want to dance, either. I want to do something else."

"You can't do that!" Veronica Grace says.

"Of course she can. What would you like to do, Kimmy?" Mrs. Aloi asks.

"I'm not sure."

"Do you play an instrument?"

"No."

"Do you like to sing?"

"No."

Mrs. Aloi looks at the clock. *LIBRARY* is next on our "Third-Grade Stars Today" list, and it happens at 10:50 whether the talent show list is done or not. "Do you have any hobbies?"

Kimmy nods. "Eating cupcakes."

Mrs. Aloi opens her mouth, then closes it. I'm pretty sure she was about to tell Kimmy that stuffing your face with cupcakes isn't a talent. But she's a teacher and part of her job is not hurting kids' feelings. "Maybe you could *make* cupcakes like on one of those TV cooking shows? You could show ingredients and demonstrate making batter."

"Ohh! I want to do that!" Kimmy claps her hands, and Mrs. Aloi writes *MAKING CUPCAKES* next to her name. "So just Veronica Grace, Isabel, and Annie for the dance extravaganza?"

Veronica Grace looks at me.

"No," I say.

Annie leans over close. "Marty, please? Just cartwheels. You don't have to dance."

"No."

"Not even for the chimps?"

She's got me there. What kind of a chimp person am I if I won't even do a few cartwheels to help buy them bananas? "Okay, fine," I say. "But no dancing. Only cartwheels. And no tiara."

"Deal," Annie says. "Mrs. Aloi, Marty's going to be in our group, too."

Mrs. Aloi raises her eyebrows at me, and I nod. She writes DANCE EXTRAVAGANZA next to my name. Looking at it makes me feel all prickly, so when Mrs. Aloi goes out into the hall to talk with Miss Gail, the art teacher, for a minute, I quick grab the marker and change it.

We finish the list right before library time, and it looks like this:

TALENT SHOW ASSIGNMENTS

VERONICA GRACE	DANCE EXTRAVAGANZA
KIMMY	MAKING CUPCAKES
EMMA	"HAPPY BIRTHDAY" — RECORDER
ISABEL	DANCE EXTRAVAGANZA
ANNIE	DANCE EXTRAVAGANZA
MARTY	~~DANCE EXTRAVAGANZA~~ just cartwheels and no tiara
ALEX	SAWING (BOARDS)
RASHEENA	HOCKEY
RUPERT	HOCKEY (GOALIE)
JIMMY	SINGING ALPHABET SONG

"Why are you singing the alphabet song?" Alex asks Jimmy on our way to the library. "That's kind of boring."

"Not when you burp the entire alphabet without taking a breath," Jimmy says, grinning.

"Whoa!" Alex says. "You can really do that?"

Jimmy nods. "I've been practicing."

"And you got Mrs. Aloi to say it was okay?" Alex looks at Jimmy in awe.

"I may have left out the burping part." Jimmy shrugs. "But I'm sure she'll love it."

chapter 4

I'm first in line at the library. "I'd like to sign out those chimpanzee books again," I tell Ms. Stephanie. I feel like I should reread them since I'm about to adopt one and everything.

Ms. Stephanie helps me find the books, but just as I'm checking them out, her phone vibrates on the counter, and she looks down. "Shoot."

"What's wrong?" I ask her.

She shakes her head. "Oh, nothing. I'm having trouble finding a place for Lady Macbeth this weekend."

"Is that your mom or something?"

Ms. Stephanie laughs. "Not quite." She pokes at her phone, and turns it to show me a picture. It's a pincushion. With a pointy-nosed face.

"Is that a baby porcupine?"

"She's my African hedgehog. I'm going away for a teaching workshop, and unfortunately, I just found out Lady Macbeth is not welcome at the doggy day care where my mom takes her poodle." She sighs.

"I'll take her!" I blurt out.

Ms. Stephanie smiles. "That's nice, Marty, but I can't ask you to —"

"No, really. Annie and I have a pet-sitting business." The words are out of my mouth before they even finish getting through my head. And it's not really a lie, even though our pet-sitting business isn't open yet, because it totally will be open as soon as I tell Annie about it. It's a perfect way to raise money for the chimps!

"We're experienced. I've helped my mom with the animals she rehabilitates, like raccoons and owls, and how different could a hedgehog be?"

"Well . . ." She's thinking about it, I can tell. "It's okay with your parents?"

"Absolutely."

"Could you take Mango and Puck, too? They're my goldfish."

"Of course!"

"What do you charge?"

"Umm . . ." I think super fast. Three pets. One dollar a pet? Or should goldfish be half price because they're so small? Or maybe like a third of the price? I should have paid attention to that fractions lesson.

"How about five dollars a day?" she says.

"That's GREAT!" I shout, and then I clap my hand over my mouth because it's still the library, even if Ms. Stephanie is the coolest librarian ever. "We're using the money to help chimpanzees at a sanctuary," I whisper.

"Sounds like a win-win situation. Shall I bring Lady Macbeth and the fish to your house tomorrow at around four?" she asks. "I don't leave for my conference until Thursday, but that will give you a chance to get to know them while I'm still around to answer questions."

"Perfect," I say. Dad won't be home yet and that's when Grandma Joyce falls asleep reading her book. "See you then!"

I grab my chimpanzee books and rush off to find Annie. Our pet-sitting business that she doesn't even know about yet already has its first customer.

chapter 5

"It is a great idea," Annie says as we walk home. "But we can't just start moving pets into your house and hope nobody notices."

"I'll get permission. We can keep them in the basement."

Annie doesn't look so sure.

"It's only two fish and a hedgehog. How much trouble could they be?"

I say good-bye to Annie and go inside for a snack. Grandma Joyce has cut up carrot sticks and made them into frilly little flowers somehow.

"How was your day?"

"Great. We're getting ready for the talent show, and I'm doing a dance with some other girls." I figure Grandma Joyce will like that.

"Lovely! I'm glad you're spending time with other young ladies."

"And we're starting a littlepetsittingbusiness." I say it really fast hoping it slides by. It doesn't.

"Pet-sitting? Marty, I don't think —"

"Only small stuff like fish," I say. *And pincushions with faces*, I think. "I'm sure Dad will say okay."

"Well, I don't think it's a good idea with your mother away." She sets down a glass of milk next to the fancy-pants carrots. "But see what your father has to say."

I wait until Grandma Joyce is busy washing tuna casserole dishes and Dad's got the Red Sox game on TV to talk to him about it. That's what Mom did when she broke the news that she was ditching us for a week to hang out with chimpanzees. Dad just nodded and never looked away from the ball game and it worked out pretty well for Mom.

"Hey, Dad . . ." I talk as fast as I can. "Annie and I want to have a pet-sitting business. It's to raise money for charity, and it's just fish and stuff. That's okay, right?"

"Sure." Dad nods and turns up the television just as somebody's bat cracks into a ball. "That's . . . ALL RIGHT!!!" He jumps up and does his Red-Sox-got-a-hit dance on top of the sofa.

"Great. Thanks!" I leave while he's happy. "Dad said yes," I tell Grandma as I pass through the kitchen and head down to set up the basement.

We have plenty of cages from Mom's job as a wildlife rehabilitator, but I figure something with a fancy name like Lady Macbeth probably has her own cage that she likes, and I bet Ms. Stephanie will bring it with her. So mostly I just pick up toys and stuff from the floor so the visiting pets don't think I'm a slob.

The doorbell rings, and Grandma Joyce calls me upstairs. It's Annie, with two melty grape Popsicles.

"Hi!" She hands me one just as it's dripping onto the floor, but Grandma swoops in with a napkin like those guys that slide into first base in Dad's baseball game.

"Why don't you girls eat those outside?" Grandma says. "Get some fresh air."

We plop down on the porch steps, and in between licks, I tell Annie about getting ready for Lady Macbeth. "Now that I've cleaned up, there's more room in our basement," I say. "So if we get more pets, we'll be able to adopt even more chimps."

Annie licks and thinks. "We need more people with pets to go on trips."

"Hey!" I jump up so fast my melty Popsicle flies off its stick onto the bottom step. There's only a little dirt on it when I pick it up, so I wipe that off on my pants and slide it back onto the stick. "Ms. Stephanie said she was going to a workshop for teachers. Maybe other teachers are going, too."

Annie's face lights up and she smiles all purple. "Other teachers with other pets! We should let them know we're available."

We finish our Popsicles and head inside.

"Hey, Dad?"

"Hi, girls! Bottom of the eighth inning." He's bouncing on the couch, wringing a pillow between his hands like it's a sponge. I hope he doesn't squeeze out the stuffing.

"We're making flyers for our —"

"Oh, come ON! If that was a strike, I'm a three-headed alien!" He looks back at us. "Sorry, what?"

"Can we use your printer?"

"YES!!!!" Dad jumps to his feet, and even though I know his yes was meant for the guy who hit the baseball, I say, "Thanks!" and pull Annie into the den.

I open up a file on the computer and write PET-SITTERS AVAILABLE at the top.

"It needs to be catchy," Annie says. " 'Going out of town? Worried about your pet? Leave your furry friends in good hands.' And then we can say prices and 'See Marty or Annie at school for more information.' "

"Think we need last names, too?"

"Nah," Annie says. "We're the only Marty and Annie. It's not like all those Sarahs."

"Perfect!" Annie says when I finish, and we print ten copies. We're going to be adopting our chimps in no time at all.

chapter 6

We go to school early on Tuesday to put up our flyers, and by lunchtime, we've got three more pets!

Our principal, Mrs. Grimes, is going to that workshop with Ms. Stephanie and wants us to watch her two hamsters.

And Mr. Klein is going to visit his sister in the hospital, so he needs somebody to babysit his parrot, Rockefeller. Mr. Klein is the custodian at our school, but he's like a teacher, too. He even comes to lunch to help with homework if you're stuck. I'm pretty sure he doesn't get paid extra for that, so the time he helped me with math, I gave him one of my Fig Newtons.

Mr. Klein shows me a picture of the parrot on his phone. "We call him Rocky for short," he says. "You know how to take care of birds?"

"Absolutely," I say.

It's not entirely true. But it will be after I do some reading, so instead of going out for recess after lunch, I head straight to the library.

"Did you finish those chimpanzee books already?" Ms. Stephanie asks.

"Not quite," I say, all out of breath. "But do you have one on parrots?"

"I think so. . . ."

"And maybe one on hamsters, too?"

She helps me find a bunch of pet-care guides and adds a stapled packet to the pile as she's checking out my books. "One more," she says. "Lady Macbeth comes with her own instructions."

"See you this afternoon at four, right?" she asks.

"Perfect," I say. The hamsters and parrot aren't coming until Thursday, so Lady Macbeth and Ms. Stephanie's fish will have plenty of time to get settled.

When I get back to the classroom with my books, it's talent show time. Everybody else is singing and burping and dancing, but I stay at my desk to read.

According to Lady Macbeth's special book, hedgehogs sleep for most of the day and run on an exercise wheel at night. Sometimes they don't even stop to go to the bathroom, so every morning, it turns out, I'm going to have to clean hedgehog poop off Lady Macbeth's running wheel. If I were Ms. Stephanie, I would have trained her to take breaks when she has to go to the bathroom. But when you are a professional pet-sitter, you don't get to decide that stuff.

"Marty, come practice with us," Annie says.

"Can't. I still have ten pages to read. Besides, I'm only doing a few cartwheels," I tell her. "I'll catch up later."

I go back to my book, but it's hard to read with all the noise. I'm the only one who hasn't gone talent show crazy today.

Alex Farley is practicing his wood-sawing act in the corner of the reading area. Only he's using an invisible imaginary saw. "If I had my saw right now, that bookcase would be in pieces," he says proudly, "but Mrs. Grimes says I can only bring it on the day of the show."

"Mrs. Aloi, can we go to the gym?" Rasheena has her hockey stick and is standing next to Rupert — at least I'm pretty sure it's Rupert. It's hard to tell because he's wearing all kinds of body pads and a goalie mask.

"Sure," Mrs. Aloi says, and turns back to the classroom. "Girls, could we turn down the music?" she calls over to Veronica Grace, Isabel, and Annie.

"Not really!" Veronica Grace shouts, spinning around. "We won't be able to hear it over Emma's recorder."

Emma is sitting on her desk, playing "Happy Birthday" over and over. Jimmy Lawson's next to her, trying to get her to play the alphabet song instead.

"I told you I don't *know* that one!" Emma says. "And stop burping!"

"Marty?" Mrs. Aloi turns to me. I'm reading pet books quietly at my desk, not burping or sawing bookshelves in half, so I can't figure out how I'm doing anything wrong. But she asks, "Shouldn't you be practicing?"

"I'm getting ready for our other adopt-a-chimp fund-raiser." I hold up the parrot book. "Pet-sitting. But I'll do some cartwheels later. Don't worry. It's going to be the best talent show ever."

Mrs. Aloi smiles and looks up, just as Isabel dances into the counter and knocks Horace's cricket container on the floor. Horace is our classroom lizard. We take turns feeding him crickets every day, and when it's your turn, you have to put the lid back on the crickets good and tight.

But somebody didn't, so the cricket lid goes flying off the jar and rolls under Isabel's desk, and crickets start hopping everywhere.

Mrs. Aloi dives for the maracas on her desk and shakes them like crazy. "Everybody! Get those crickets!"

Everyone stops being talented and drops to the floor to chase crickets. When we finally get the last one back in the jar, Mrs. Aloi screws on the top super tight and sinks into her chair.

"That was awesome!" Jimmy Lawson says. "Hey! We should do cricket catching as a class talent. We could let them all go onstage and then —"

Mrs. Aloi's maracas interrupt him. "Time to write down assignments and pack up to go home!" she shouts.

She sounds like she is already overwhelmed by all our talent.

Annie comes over after school, and at exactly four o'clock, the doorbell rings.

"I'll get it! It's one of my friends," I add so Grandma won't feel like she has to put her book down and get up from the couch in the living room.

Ms. Stephanie is at the door with her arms wrapped around her goldfish bowl. Mango and Puck are zipping around in circles. "Here you go," she says, handing me the bowl. "I'll be right back with Lady Macbeth."

I get Mango and Puck settled in the basement playroom on top of my old dresser with the missing drawer handles, and Ms. Stephanie comes downstairs with a big wire cage that she eases onto the dresser next to the fish. Lady Macbeth's cage has an exercise wheel, food and water dishes, and a little igloo cave inside. Annie is carrying Lady Macbeth in a cozy thing that looks like a tiny dog bed.

"She's a sweetheart, but she doesn't like to be awake in the daytime much," Ms. Stephanie says. She reaches into the little hedgehog bed, cups her hands carefully around Lady Macbeth's prickles, and lifts her up to meet us.

"Hi there," I whisper.

Lady Macbeth puffs herself up and makes this weird sharp sniffing sound, and I take a step back. "She's chuffing," Ms. Stephanie says. "She does that when she's upset."

Prickles look even more prickly on an upset hedgehog.

Ms. Stephanie opens the door of the big wire cage and sets the hedgehog very gently inside. Lady Macbeth takes one look at us and disappears into the igloo cave.

"She'll get used to you," Ms. Stephanie says. "Did you have a chance to read through her care manual?"

"Every last page."

"Great." Ms. Stephanie looks at her watch. "I'd better go. Stop by the library tomorrow if you have questions."

We figure maybe when Ms. Stephanie leaves, Lady Macbeth will come out to play a little. But she stays in her cave.

I lean my head close. "I can still hear her huffing and chuffing in there."

"Look on the bright side," Annie says. "She'll leave us lots of time to play with the other pets."

Chuff!

chapter 7

We get another pet-sitting job at recess on Wednesday.

"Excuse me." A skinny first-grade girl tugs my sleeve as I'm about to climb the monkey bars. "Are you Marty who pet-sits?"

"Yes, I am. What's your name?"

"Sarah." She gives me a serious look through her bangs. "I need you to take Joyce for a few days."

"Okay. My grandma's name is Joyce, too. Who's your Joyce?"

"She's right here." She reaches into her pocket and pulls out a shiny creamy-tan slug about half the size of her pinkie finger.

"Does she have a cage or anything?"

"I was keeping her on some leaves in the sugar bowl, but my dad wanted it back for sugar."

I nod. "Parents are like that sometimes."
But where will I keep her until I get home?
Joyce might get smushed in my pocket, so I
hold her in my palm for now. "The thing is . . .
we're actually charging money for pet-sitting.
It's for a good cause," I add, "to help rescued
chimpanzees."

Sarah nods, digs into her other pocket, and
pulls out a nickel and six pennies. "It's not more
than this, is it?"

"No," I decide. "You're in luck. We're having a sale on slug-sitting, so this is plenty. How long do you need us to keep Joyce?"

"Until my slug house is finished. Miss Gail is helping me make one out of clay," she says, and skips off to the swings, leaving me with slimy Joyce in my hand.

After recess, I sneak back into the cafeteria and find a plastic bag with lettuce in it from somebody's sandwich. I drop Joyce in there, leave the top open so she can breathe, and put the bag in my desk until it's time to go home.

Before school Thursday morning, I take more pet-sitting notes from my books.

Things are going well so far. I put Joyce in one of Dad's coffee mugs with some leaves from the garden. She hangs out leaving slime trails and seems happy.

I haven't seen Lady Macbeth out of her cave,

but she must have a lot of fun at night because her running wheel was a mess this morning. I cleaned it and put it back just like the directions said.

Annie knocks on the door. I know it's her because we're supposed to walk to school together. "Come on in!" I call. "I'm studying." I hold up the hamster guide.

She reaches for the parrot book. "Are you done with this one?"

"Yeah." I drink what's left of the milk from my cereal bowl. "The parrot's going to be tough. It says you have to give them lots of attention or they get mean. I think we might need more help."

"I bet Rupert and Alex would come over sometimes," Annie says.

"Let's ask Rasheena, too." I load the rest of the pet books into my backpack and we head to school.

"You're babysitting a parrot?" Alex says when Annie and I find him at recess. "That's awesome! Can it talk?"

"I don't know." I didn't ask Mr. Klein, but that would be neat.

"Count me in," Alex says.

"I'd love to help," Rasheena says.

"Me, too," Rupert says, "as long as the animals stay at your house. My mom won't even let us get a fish."

Everybody promises to come over before Rocky the parrot arrives at four, and then Annie heads for the playground to meet Veronica Grace and Isabel. "Marty, you should practice with us today. The talent show's in five days, and you haven't even seen the routine yet."

"Not today," I say, and hold up the hamster book. "Gotta study!"

Right before the bell rings to go home, I hear Mrs. Grimes coming down the hall in her clickety-clackety shoes. They clickety-clack right up to our classroom door, and there she is, carrying a wire cage with two yellow-gold fluffballs huddled inside.

"Marty! Annie! I'm glad I caught you. I have a late meeting today, so I won't be able to come by your house. May I give you the hamsters now?"

"We'd be delighted," I say, because that sounds more professional than "You betcha!"

"Wonderful." She hoists the cage onto a desk, along with a bag of food and wood chips and stuff. "Here's everything you'll need. Please clean up their droppings and add bedding to the cage as needed. They get fresh food and water every morning. And long-haired hamsters should be brushed daily." She rummages through the bag. "Oh dear, I've forgotten their brush, but an old toothbrush will work just fine."

"I'm sure we have one," I say, bending down to look in the cage. The hamsters have shiny black eyes like polished pebbles, and their yellowy fur looks so soft. I can't wait to hold them. "What are their names?"

"Fluffernutter and Houdini." Mrs. Grimes looks proud. "I should warn you. Houdini's name suits him very well. He's named for a famous magician who always —"

The bell rings then, and Mrs. Grimes jumps like somebody poked her with a pin. "Oh! I have to do announcements." She pauses at the door. "You do know how to care for hamsters, right?"

"Every detail." I hold up my hamster library book and smile. Mrs. Grimes gives me a thumbs-up and clickety-clacks back down the hall. A minute later, we hear her voice over the loud-speaker, reminding us about homework passes and kickball intramurals and chicken nuggets for lunch tomorrow.

"And don't forget," she says, "just four days until our third-grade talent show! I hope you've all been practicing."

Annie gives me a look.

"I've been busy," I say. "Let's go. We've got two hamsters to take care of and a parrot on the way in half an hour."

chapter 8

When Annie and I get to my house, Grandma's right in the kitchen, so we leave Fluffernutter and Houdini on the porch at first. It's part of our plan.

"Hello, girls!" Grandma Joyce says. "Ready for a snack?"

"Yep. I just need to use the bathroom." I hurry upstairs, dig out some dirt from my pocket, and sprinkle it under the sink. "Uh-oh! Grandma?" I call. "I think there might be mouse droppings up here!"

I hear some fumbling in the kitchen, and then Grandma Joyce tears up the stairs with her cleaning fluid and a roll of paper towels. From the top of the stairs, I motion for Annie to grab the hamster cage and move it down to the basement.

Annie and I are eating molasses cookies at the kitchen table by the time Grandma comes back.

"Just a little dirt." Grandma brushes off her hands and tosses a muddy paper towel into the trash.

"We're going downstairs to play, okay? And . . . is it all right if a couple more friends come over to study spelling and stuff?"

"Of course!" Grandma reaches for her mixing bowl. "I'll make more cookies."

By five minutes to four, Rupert, Alex, and Rasheena have arrived. Grandma's new cookies are warm out of the oven, and she's reading her book at the kitchen table. Rupert, Annie, Alex, Rasheena, and I take our cookies out to the porch to wait for Mr. Klein.

"I put the hamster cage on the edge of that big dresser with the fish and Lady Macbeth," Annie says, plopping down onto the top porch step, "but then Lady Macbeth did that scary chuffing-puffing thing, so I moved the hamsters to the bookshelf. Where are we going to put the parrot?"

"You could make a backyard aviary for it. Mick Buzzsaw built one on *Handyman America* once," Alex says, ducking under the porch railing and jumping down to the sidewalk. He looks into our backyard. "You've got plenty of room."

"Yeah, only Dad and Grandma don't exactly know about the parrot," I say. "And Grandma's

still in the kitchen. We need to figure out a way to sneak him into the basement."

"Better get figuring," Annie says, pointing down the street at a white pickup truck. When it stops at our house, Mr. Klein hops out of the driver's seat, jogs to the passenger's side, and pulls out a big birdcage with a dark blue sheet draped over it.

"That's going to be tough to hide," Rasheena says.

"We can't go through the house." I turn to Annie. "You know the door that goes from our basement out to the backyard? Can you run and open it?"

She hurries inside while Rasheena, Rupert, Alex, and I go down to meet Mr. Klein on the sidewalk.

"This is quite a welcoming committee," he says, grinning.

"Hi, Mr. Klein!" I say. "We're excited to meet Rocky."

"Let's get him inside." He starts up the front steps.

"You can't go that way!" I blurt.

Mr. Klein stops. "What?"

"He's staying in our basement playroom, and it's . . . much easier to get there the back way," I say. *Because then you don't have to get past Grandma Joyce*, I think.

"Okay." Mr. Klein follows us around the house to the back door. I hold my breath when we go past the big living room window. But when I peek inside, the couch is empty. Grandma must still be in the kitchen.

When we get to the basement, Mr. Klein sets down Rocky's cage and pulls off the blue sheet.

"Wow! He's beautiful!" I thought parrots were green, but this one has a white face with round yellow-and-black eyes. Rocky's body is all gray like smooth lake rocks, except for a super bright tail so red it looks like it's on fire.

"Look at his beak!" Annie squeals. It's all black and sharp and hooked.

"Check out those feet!" Rupert says, leaning in close. They're all scaly and curled and talony.

"That is one cool bird," Rasheena says, and lets out a whistle.

The parrot whistles right back at her, and Mr. Klein laughs. "He's a bit of a copycat."

"Can he talk?" Annie leans in close to the bird. "Polly want a cracker. Polly want a cracker?"

"Back off," squawks the parrot, and then it calls Annie a name I've only heard once, when my dad was really mad at another driver who backed into our minivan in the Shop-a-Lot parking lot. Mom gave Dad her you-are-in-big-trouble-mister look, so I'm guessing it's a pretty bad word. When I look at Mr. Klein, I know I'm right because his face is as red as Rocky's tail.

"Uh . . . sorry," he mumbles, and then shrugs. "My buddy Tom was visiting last week. Looks

like he taught Rocky some new vocabulary. The guy curses like a sailor." He shakes his head and gives the bird a frown. "Watch your language."

"Watch your language," Rocky repeats, and then calls Mr. Klein the bad parking-lot name.

"We'll try to teach him to say other stuff," Annie promises.

Mr. Klein clears his throat and pulls a crumpled piece of notebook paper from his pocket. "Here's what you'll need to do each day. Change the newspaper in his cage and give him fresh food and water. It's only a few days, so you don't need to clean the cage, but please spend plenty of time with him so he doesn't get lonely."

Rupert gives a salute. "We're pros, Mr. Klein. No problem."

"We'll talk to him all the time," I say.

"Great." Mr. Klein heads for the door but then turns back. "Promise me one more thing. Whatever he says, don't repeat it in front of your parents."

chapter 9

Two hamsters, one parrot, a hedgehog, two fish, and a slug didn't sound like too many animals to babysit for a few days. But even with everybody helping on Friday morning, it feels like we'll never get our pet jobs done in time for school.

"I don't want to be in charge of the grouchy hedgehog!" Alex holds up Ms. Stephanie's care manual. "It would take me a year to read this whole thing."

"Fine. I'll do the hedgehog," I say, handing him the fish food. "You feed Mango and Puck."

Alex dumps a bunch of food into their bowl, so much that a thick layer of it covers the whole top of the water like a fish-food blanket.

"That's too much!" I scoop most of it up with

my hand and try to get it back in the container, even though it's all soggy now. "They only need about ten flakes." I wipe my hand on my jeans, but my fingers still smell like fish-food-mush.

"Marty, I'm going to feed this lettuce to the parrot, okay?" Rupert calls from across the room.

"Sure. Vegetables are fine for parrots."

"Oh, gross!" he says. "It's got a big booger on it or something."

"Joyce!!" I scream, and snatch the slug cup out of his hand just as he's opening Rocky's birdcage.

"What?!" Grandma hollers from the kitchen.

"Not you!" I yell. "I mean . . . never mind!"

"Since when do you call me by my first name?" she calls down the stairs.

"Sorry, Grandma!" I put the slug cup back on the bookshelf and announce, "This is not food. It is a pet."

"Somebody has a pet booger?" Alex says.

"It's a slug. She belongs to Sarah-the-first-grader."

Rasheena looks down into the coffee cup. "What do slugs eat?"

"I'm not positive," I admit. "I couldn't find a book on slugs, but I looked them up on the computer, and it said they eat garden plants. Maybe we can just give her more lettuce. Sarah didn't leave instructions."

"Well, Mrs. Grimes did," Annie says. "And we need to brush the hamsters. Did you find an old toothbrush?"

"I'll check." I hurry upstairs. Grandma's outside watering flowers, so I go straight to the upstairs bathroom. My red toothbrush is there next to Dad's blue one on the sink. Mom's yellow one is gone — she took it with her to the chimp sanctuary — but in the medicine cabinet, there's an extra bright green one. I grab that and run back downstairs.

"Here." I hand Annie the toothbrush, and she starts brushing the hamsters, first Fluffernutter and then Houdini. "Houdini's a weird name for a hamster," she says.

"Sounds like something my grandma would make with marinara sauce and Parmesan cheese," Alex says.

"I'm hungry," Rupert says. "Got any bagels?"

"We don't have time," I say. "Alex, can you

feed the parrot?" I hand him the birdseed Mr. Klein left us. "Start with this, and I'll find him some vegetables."

I run upstairs and almost crash into Grandma Joyce in the kitchen. "It's about time," she says. "Aren't your friends coming?" She eyes the basement door and heads that way.

"Grandma, please don't —"

"Get moving, kids!" she hollers down the stairs. "It's time for school!"

For a couple seconds, nobody answers. Then Rocky breaks the quiet.

"Back off!" he screeches.

No, no, no, I think.

But he squawks that bad parking-lot word up the stairs, clear as can be.

Grandma Joyce turns slowly toward me. Her voice is super calm. Scary calm. "What. Did. I. Just. Hear?"

"That . . . was Alex," I say. Grandma's

eyebrows go up so high they disappear into her gray curls. I shake my head like Mr. Klein did. "The guy curses like a sailor."

"Tell your friend to watch his language."

"I'll tell them to hurry up, too," I say, and rush back downstairs. Rupert has taken over hedgehog duty, so Lady Macbeth has fresh food and water and is huddled in her igloo cave. Her running wheel only looks a little poopy; I'll clean it when I get home. Fish are fed. Hamsters brushed. And the slug . . .

I look around for the coffee cup, but somebody moved it. "Has anybody seen the slug cup?"

"This?" Rasheena holds up the cup. It's empty.

"Where's Joyce?"

"Where's Joyce? Where's Joyce?" the parrot screeches.

"I'm up here where you should be, getting ready for school!" Grandma yells down.

"Coming!" I shout up the stairs, and whip back around to Rasheena. "Where's the lettuce that was in that cup?"

"Oh!" Rupert snaps his fingers, rushes to the couch, and picks up a pillow. The lettuce is piled on it, and Joyce is perched on top like it's some kind of ruffly slug bed. "Sorry, I needed the cup to get water for the hedgehog."

"I'm almost done with the hamsters." Annie slow-walks across the room with a bowl of water for Fluffernutter and Houdini.

"Did anybody get water for the parrot?" I ask.

"Yeah. That thing tried to bite me, too." Alex glares into Rocky's cage.

"Knock it off, stupid jerk. Knock it off, stupid jerk," the parrot squawks.

"Alex has been teaching the parrot new words," Annie says. "Can somebody help me with the top of this hamster cage? It feels kind of loose."

"Do I have to come down there?" Grandma hollers. "Let's go!"

"It's fine," I tell Annie, and rush upstairs.

We make it to school just as the bell rings, and I sink into my seat. My face is all sweaty and sticky. My fingers smell like fish-food-mush, and no way can I concentrate on fractions. Pet-sitting is way harder than I thought it would be. When you can't even count on the slug to stay put, you know it's going to be a long few days.

chapter 10

After morning classwork, when it's time for talent show practice, Jimmy Lawson shows up with cymbals borrowed from the music room.

"Wait a minute," Mrs. Aloi says, checking her talent list. "Aren't you singing the alphabet song? There are no cymbals in the alphabet song."

"I'm doing an original version," he says.

Rupert and Rasheena have taken over one half of the classroom with their hockey net, so Jimmy takes his cymbals, pushes past Veronica Grace, Isabel, and Annie practicing their dance, and heads for the far reading corner where Horace hangs out. I can hear Jimmy burping his letters really quietly, and then he smashes the symbols during the pauses.

"A-B-C-D-E-F-G . . .
Crash! H-I-J-K-L-M-N-
O-P . . . *Crash!*"

Every time Jimmy
smashes the cymbals
together, poor Horace
jumps about a mile.

"Mrs. Aloi, do you have an
egg I can borrow?" Kimmy
calls from the desk where
she's been practicing her
cupcake-baking demonstration.

"An egg?"

Kimmy points to the floor. "Mine all rolled
off the desk and broke."

"Oh dear," Mrs. Aloi says. "There are paper
towels over in the —"

"Hey, can I practice sawing on your desk?" Alex
rushes up with a pretend saw he's cut out of card-

board, but he slips on egg goo and goes flailing through Veronica Grace, Isabel, and Annie's dance.

"Alex! You totally messed us up!" Veronica Grace stomps her sparkly tap shoe on the floor. "Now we have to start over."

"Marty, will you practice with us?" Annie asks.

"I will later." I hold up the parrot book. "I want to read this again to make sure we're feeding Rocky the right stuff."

"But today's our last chance before Monday," Annie says.

Veronica Grace shrugs. "We don't need her. I can do cartwheels, and if she's not going to practice, she shouldn't get to be in the extravaganza."

"I didn't want to be in your dumb dance thing anyway," I say.

"It's an *extravaganza*," Veronica Grace says.

"I *especially* don't want to be in that. Mrs. Aloi, I'm going to do something else for the talent show. Please cross me off the dance recital."

"Extravaganza!" Veronica Grace stomps her foot.

"Whatever," I say. And I plop down with my book.

Annie waits for me to walk to lunch. "I was thinking . . . maybe Mrs. Baxter needs a pet-sitter," she says. "She has a hermit crab, remember? When Rasheena went to Florida last year, Mrs. Baxter asked her to bring back a new shell for it."

"Maybe." I'm a little mad at Annie since Veronica Grace kicked me out of the dance extravaganza. It's not like I wanted to be in it, but it would have been nice if Annie had stuck up for me. But I kind of like Mrs. Baxter the cafeteria lady. "I'll check with her when I get my milk."

"Skim, two percent, or chocolate?" Mrs. Baxter says when I come through the line.

"Chocolate, please. And I was wondering . . ." I pause, thinking about how crazy it's been trying to take care of all the pets. Do we really want another one? But then I remember the chimps. "I was wondering if you needed any help pet-sitting this week."

"Seriously?" She tips her head. I guess it was a weird question to ask out of nowhere.

"Well, it's just that we're raising money to help these chimps, and we're taking care of some other pets, so . . ."

"Isn't that something! I've been looking for somebody willing to take Bitsy for a day or two so I can visit my sister. You sure it's okay with your folks?"

"Of course. I take care of lots of small pets."

"Oh, Bitsy's not so small anymore."

"That's okay." I wonder how big Bitsy's shell is now. "We've got tons of space. She has her own cage, right?"

"Sure does."

"Great!" I add Bitsy the hermit crab to the

list of pets in my head. "We usually charge five dollars a day. All the money goes to charity. Can you bring Bitsy to my house after school around four?"

"Works for me," Mrs. Baxter says. She slips me a chocolate chip cookie, even though you're only supposed to get them if you buy the hot lunch, and I'm very, very glad I decided to ask about her crab. I've got another pet to sit, another ten dollars for chimp adoption, *and* an extra dessert.

chapter 11

After school, Annie, Rupert, Rasheena, and Alex come over to help me get ready for Bitsy.

"If we move the hedgehog over, there's room on the dresser," Annie says.

"Yeah, but Lady Macbeth chuffs at everything," I say. "I don't want her to scare Bitsy." I drag in the plastic table that Dad uses for folding laundry in the other part of the basement. "We can put her cage on here."

"Hey, wait a minute . . ." Rasheena's looking into the hedgehog cage. "Lady Macbeth is coming out of her cave. Think she wants to play?"

I rush over because it's the first time I've seen Lady Macbeth since she got here. Annie and Rupert and Alex come, too. Lady Macbeth takes one look up at us and tucks her head into her body until it disappears. She looks like a turtle with a super spiky shell.

"Well, that was exciting," Rupert says, and goes to visit Rocky. "Try saying this . . . 'Rupert is awesome. Rupert rocks.' "

Rocky turns away and poops on the newspaper on the bottom of his cage. Which reminds me. "I'm supposed to put fresh paper in Rocky's cage every day."

I run upstairs, grab a newspaper from the kitchen table, and bring it down. "Do you think Rocky would like to go to the bathroom on the front page, comics, arts section, or sports pages?"

"Sports," Alex says. "That's the section my dad always takes when he goes to the bathroom. And be careful." Alex hasn't gone near the parrot since he got nipped.

I line Rocky's cage with the sports section. He doesn't try to bite me or anything. "I think he likes me," I tell Alex. "And I bet Lady Macbeth will, too, once we spend some time together." I go back to her cage. She's still all turtled up in a prickly ball, but I reach in slowly and cup my hands around her body the way I saw Ms. Stephanie do.

"Careful," Annie says. "She's chuffing again."

"She'll be happier once she gets to know us." I put Lady Macbeth down on the carpet, and we all plop down around her.

"Hey there, pincushion," Alex says.

"Well, that's just going to make her mad," Rasheena says.

"Maybe it's a compliment if you're a hedgehog," Rupert says. "You never know."

Lady Macbeth quiets down, and her pointy nose sticks out a tiny bit.

"Hold out your hand so she can sniff it," Alex says. "That's what we do to introduce my dog to strangers."

I try that, only my hand is big enough to cover Lady Macbeth's whole head, and that can't feel very friendly, so I hold two fingers up to her nose. She sticks her head out a little farther.

"See?" Alex says. "I think she's —"

"YeeeeeOWWW!" Little hedgehog teeth clamp down on the edge of my finger — and they are sharp things, let me tell you — so I quick tug my hand back. But Lady Macbeth doesn't let go, so I sort of drag her across the carpet.

"Careful!" Annie says, and holds my hand still until Lady Macbeth unclamps her teeth and waddles away.

I look down at my finger. There's no blood. "Can somebody put her back in her cage?"

Annie looks at Rupert. Rupert looks at Alex. Alex looks at Rasheena. "Oh, fine," she says. "Do you have any gloves or anything?"

All we can find is a pair of my old snow mittens, so Rasheena squeezes her hands into those and gets Lady Macbeth back in her cage.

She's chuffing again. Or maybe laughing. It's hard to tell.

Then the doorbell rings.

"I forgot to tell Mrs. Baxter to come to the back door!" I fly up the stairs. Grandma's nowhere to be found.

"Marty, I'm in the ladies' room. Could you be a dear and answer the door?" she calls.

Saved! I rush to the door and fling it open. Mrs. Baxter is standing there with . . . empty hands.

"Didn't you bring Bitsy?" I ask.

"Oh yes," she says. "She's in the car, but her cage is pretty big. I wanted to make sure you're all set before we bring it in."

"Yeah, we have a whole table for her," I say, wondering just how big a cage for a hermit crab could be. "Can you bring her cage to the back door so we can get it down to the basement playroom?"

"That's fine," Mrs. Baxter says, "but I'll need some help."

"Okay," I say, and start for the car.

But Mrs. Baxter looks past me into the house. "It'll take more than the two of us."

"It will?" Seriously? How big could that cage be? Either Mrs. Baxter thinks I'm a total weakling or she's spoiling Bitsy with some kind of hermit crab mansion. But she's the customer, so I say, "I'll get my friends."

Mrs. Baxter walks toward her car. When I come back with Annie, Alex, Rupert, and Rasheena, she smiles and opens the door to the backseat. "Kids," she says, "meet my Bitsy."

We all stare.

Mrs. Baxter was right. It's a super-sized cage, longer than I am tall.

But it's no hermit crab mansion. Because Bitsy is not a hermit crab.

Not even close.

chapter 12

Bitsy is a Burmese python.

Bitsy is six feet long and as big around as a grapefruit.

Bitsy eats live rodents for dinner.

"But I brought you a frozen mouse to feed her," Mrs. Baxter says, smiling. "That'll be easier."

Alex looks at his wrist where a watch would be if he had one. Maybe it's an imaginary watch. "Wow. I have to go. I promised my mom I'd be home by five."

Mrs. Baxter looks at her watch. Hers is real. "It's only four."

"Yeah . . . well . . ." Alex is already buckling his bicycle helmet. "She worries if I'm late." He jumps on his bike and takes off down the sidewalk.

"I don't think Alex likes Bitsy," Rasheena says, squatting down to look through the glass of the cage. "She's really pretty if you look close."

Mrs. Baxter's face lights up. "Isn't she? I know some people are afraid of snakes, but Bitsy has been handled since she was a baby and she's so gentle with people. She's a wonderful companion. I was heartbroken when Big Bubba died."

"Big Bubba?" Rupert says.

"My hermit crab. He was a cute little guy."

"Oh." Rupert looks into the tank, and I know what he's thinking. Bitsy looks a whole lot more like a Big Bubba than a Bitsy. But I guess you can't just go naming all your pets "Big Bubba." You'd have to have Big Bubba the First, Big Bubba the Second, Big Bubba the —

"Let's get her inside, okay?" Mrs. Baxter reaches into the car and pulls out one end of Bitsy's cage. "Everybody grab a corner."

The cage is heavy, but together, we get it out of the car. I hold my breath while we walk past the big living room window, but when I sneak a look inside, Grandma Joyce is on the couch reading her book and never looks up. Not even when we walk by with a ginormous snake. That must be a seriously good book.

We carry Bitsy down the basement stairs and get her set up on the laundry table. "It's a little wobbly," Mrs. Baxter says.

"I think it's meant more for matching socks than holding snakes," I say. "Should we put the cage on the floor instead?"

Mrs. Baxter shakes her head. "No, it might get drafty down there. The table will be fine. Just be careful not to bump into it. Bitsy doesn't like to be jostled." She looks around the room and walks up to the parrot's cage. "Polly want a cracker?"

"Stupid jerk," the parrot says.

Mrs. Baxter laughs. "Well, aren't you feisty! What else can you say?"

"Back off —"

I jump between Rocky and Mrs. Baxter. "Isn't he the greatest?!" I shout, loud enough to drown out what Rocky says next.

"He seems like a real character," Mrs. Baxter says.

"He sure is." Annie takes Mrs. Baxter's arm and leads her away from Rocky's cage, back to Bitsy. "Is there anything else we should know?"

"Oh!" Mrs. Baxter snaps her fingers and runs out the door. She comes back with a big purple purse and pulls out a plastic baggie. Inside is something that looks like the moldy half pork chop Grandma Joyce found when she was cleaning out the back of our fridge on Sunday.

"Bitsy's dinner for tomorrow. One frozen mouse."

"So . . . we just drop it in the cage?" I ask. I feel kind of bad for the mouse.

"You may need to tie a string to it and jerk it around a bit so she'll eat it. She likes live rodents best, but I thought this would be simpler."

"Definitely."

"Keep the light on so she doesn't get cold. I'll fetch her water dish. I took it out of the cage so it wouldn't slosh around."

"We'll come get it." I follow Mrs. Baxter outside. The sooner we get her away from Rocky, the better.

"Thanks so much, kids." Mrs. Baxter reaches into her backseat and hands me a shallow water dish, then climbs into her car. "It's not easy to find a Bitsy-sitter, you know."

We wave to Mrs. Baxter as she pulls away from the curb.

"Would you have volunteered to be a Bitsy-sitter if you'd known what Bitsy was?" Rasheena asks.

"Maybe not," I say, heading back downstairs with the water dish. I lift the lid to her tank just a little, waiting to see what she does. But Bitsy stays curled in one corner, all shiny and coiled-up cozy. Her skin is a patchy brown-beige-green. Slowly, I lower the water into the open space on the other side of the tank.

"I thought Mrs. Grimes had two hamsters," Rupert says from across the room.

"She does," I hear Annie say. "That's Fluffernutter with the orange spot by her ear, and . . . uh-oh."

"'Uh-oh'?" I pull my arm out of Bitsy's tank so fast my elbow gets caught on the lid, and the part that lifts up breaks right off and clatters to the floor. I pick it up, shove it back onto the tank, and rush to the hamster cage. Houdini is missing. "How could he have gotten out?"

"Maybe he's hiding." Annie pokes around the wood shavings in the corners of the cage, but there's no Houdini. "Oh no! I thought that lid might have been on wrong this morning."

"He must be around somewhere." Rasheena squats to check under the futon.

I look under the heating vent on the floor.

"Will you look in the laundry room?" I ask Rupert. "I'm going upstairs to make sure he didn't get up to the living room. Grandma Joyce would flip."

"I'll check the kitchen," Annie says. "Maybe he was hungry."

"I'll make sure all your doors are closed," Rasheena says. "As long as he doesn't get out of the house, he'll turn up."

I look under the TV stand and under Dad's

big puffy chair in the living room. I crawl past Grandma and look under the couch.

"What did you lose, Marty?"

"Um . . . sometimes my LEGO pieces bounce under here." That's technically true. Even though what I lost this time is fluffier than a LEGO.

"Well, I vacuumed thoroughly under there today. I hope I didn't suck it up. You should be more careful with your things."

I picture Houdini being swallowed up with the potato chip crumbs and dust, and I run to the closet where we keep the vacuum cleaner. I squat down and press my ear to the bag. There's no scratching or anything, so I go to the kitchen to see how Annie's doing.

She shakes her head. "No luck."

Rasheena comes in from the front hallway with Rupert. He's all linty from crawling around the laundry room.

"No sign of Houdini," Rasheena says. "But

I don't think he could have gotten out of the house."

Boy, I hope she's right. "Let's check the basement again. Maybe he's hiding."

Annie nods. "He's probably scared."

I hurry downstairs and go right to the hamster cage, hoping Houdini decided to go home on his own. But there's only Fluffernutter, sitting by the water dish, looking lonely. I reach in to scratch her head.

"Marty?" Annie's voice trembles. She must be really worried about Houdini. "We have a problem."

"No kidding," I say, turning around. "Maybe we should —"

The look on her face makes me stop talking.

And when I look past her, I know our problem is bigger than a missing hamster.

Much, much bigger.

chapter 13

The broken lid of Bitsy's tank is sort of shoved to one side.

The water dish is where I left it when I ran over to the hamster cage.

But Bitsy is gone.

We look all over the basement.

"Not in the laundry room," Rupert calls.

"Not under the futon," says Rasheena.

We run out of ideas pretty fast. There are only so many places a six-foot-long python can hide.

"Not behind the dresser," Annie says. "Marty, what if she got upstairs?"

I take a deep breath and head for the kitchen. Grandma's making three-bean Mexican casserole and she hasn't screamed, so I know Bitsy isn't in there.

We look under all the beds in all the bedrooms and under the sleeper sofa in the guest room where Grandma's staying.

No snake.

No hamster.

Not even a LEGO piece.

"Bitsy's got to be somewhere," Rasheena says, plopping down on the living room couch. "We were only gone five or ten minutes."

"Maybe we should call Mrs. Baxter," Annie says.

"And tell her we lost her snake? Are you kidding?"

"But maybe Bitsy's gotten away before," Annie says. "Maybe Mrs. Baxter knows where snakes like to hide."

"Wait a minute!" I jump up from the floor. "We can look that up on my dad's computer. Some snake somewhere must have gotten out of its cage before, and maybe its owner wrote about where they found it. Grandma!" I call into the kitchen. "Okay if we use the computer for a project?"

I hear dishes clanking. "Sure. Let me know if you need help."

We huddle around the computer, and I quick type *WHERE DO SNAKES LIKE TO HANG OUT* in the search box.

The pages that come up all have pictures of swamps and rocky caves and stuff.

"This is about where they live in the wild," Annie says.

I remember what Ms. Stephanie taught us about using keywords and being specific, and I try again.

PET PYTHON ESCAPED WHERE TO SEARCH

This time, we find an article written by a guy who has a whole mess of pet snakes. "Bad news,"

Annie says, reading over my shoulder. "Even big snakes can squeeze into tiny spaces. She could be anywhere. This guy says to check kitchen cabinets."

I shake my head. "If Bitsy was in a kitchen cabinet, Grandma would have found her by now."

"What about this?" Rasheena points to the next paragraph. "It says you can set noise traps by putting crinkly plastic bags all around the house in places the snake might go. Like behind furniture and underneath couches and stuff. And then when it gets dark, sit really quietly and listen to see if you hear it moving."

A tingle goes through me because a big snake in the dark doesn't sound good at all. Even if she is as gentle as Mrs. Baxter promised, she's still ginormous. But we have to try something. "That might work," I say, "especially since Grandma did our grocery shopping this week." Mom hates plastic and has reusable bags, but I saw some of those plastic Shop-a-Lot bags in the kitchen earlier. "Anything else?"

"It says you can sprinkle a strip of flour or cornstarch in all your doorways before you go to bed at night," Rasheena says. "Then if the snake moves from room to room in the middle of the night, it'll leave a trail."

"Oh." I hadn't thought about Bitsy slithering into my bedroom at night. I liked Bitsy better in her cage.

Annie, Rupert, and Rasheena stay for dinner and more cookies, and then Grandma cleans up the kitchen and settles on the couch with her book. When Dad joins her and turns on the baseball game, we put Operation Snake Trap into effect.

"The website said to put one behind every bookshelf, dresser, and large household appliance," I say, handing out plastic bags. "Under couches and chairs, too."

Rupert takes some bags and peers into the living room. "What if your dad and grandma ask why I'm shoving plastic bags under the couch?"

I think about this for a minute. "The Red Sox are on, so Dad probably won't notice. But if Grandma asks, tell her it's a science experiment."

Rupert hurries into the living room. Annie and Rasheena set sound traps all over the kitchen, while I haul a five-pound bag of flour upstairs and hide it under my bed. By then it's getting dark and everybody has to go home.

"Good luck," Annie says as she walks down the porch steps.

I go inside and search the house one more time. "Houdini?" I whisper under chairs. "Bitsy?"

Nobody answers.

I kiss Dad and Grandma good night, brush my teeth and put on my pajamas, and read my chimpanzee book in bed.

"Has anybody seen my toothbrush?" Grandma calls.

"What color is it?" I yell from my room.

"Green."

"Haven't seen it," Dad says. While they're looking to see if we have extras in the other bathroom, I race down to the basement. The green toothbrush is on the floor by the hamster cage. I grab it and pick off as many hairs as I can on my way upstairs. Grandma and Dad get back to the bathroom while I'm rinsing it under the sink.

"There it is!" Grandma says. "Where was it?"

"It fell on the floor," I say. Which is totally true. She doesn't ask which floor. "It got a little dirty."

Grandma looks at it. "I'll rinse it some more."

"Good idea," I say, and go to bed.

I wait until she finishes rinsing and brushing and goes to bed. When I hear Dad's door close, too, I get up and pull the bag of flour from under my bed. A big powdery cloud puffs out when I open it, but I wave it away and get to work.

I pour a nice thick line of flour across every doorway in the house.

Then I go down to the living room and listen for a while. Nothing scratches. Nothing crinkles. So I go back to bed.

I dream about giant, six-foot hamsters and fluffy snakes all night long. Every time I wake up, I think the same thing. Please, please, *please* let me find Houdini and Bitsy before Mrs. Grimes and Mrs. Baxter come back to pick them up.

chapter 14

"Marty?" Dad's voice wakes me up Saturday morning.

"Hi, Dad." It's really light out. I must have slept in. "What time is it?"

"Time for you to get cleaning." He's standing in my doorway with his coffee mug, wearing his old green bathrobe and brown slippers. They're smudged white on the toes.

"Oh!" I remember my flour traps and jump out of bed. I rush past him to the hallway, but there are no Bitsy tracks. Just big slipper-prints leading out of Mom and Dad's room through the hall and down the stairs. They're almost invisible by the time they get to the bottom step. "Dad tracks." I sigh.

"What were you expecting — Godzilla?" He

stands in my doorway, hands on his hips. "You need to clean this up. Mom comes home tomorrow."

"I know." Ms. Stephanie, whose hedgehog hates me, will be back tomorrow, too. So will Mr. Klein, whose parrot will probably call him a stupid jerk since Alex taught him even more rude things. Mrs. Grimes will be back for her two hamsters and will find out we lost one. And Mrs. Baxter will be back to get Bitsy, and Bitsy's gone, too.

"Oohhh!" I flop back on my bed, bury my face in the pillow, and squeeze my eyes shut.

"Hey, kiddo." I feel Dad's hand on my back. "Relax. It's just a little flour. And I bet Grandma will help you vacuum. You know how good she is at that stuff."

I take a big breath of pillow-air. Then I sit up. "It's not just a little flour," I say.

And I tell Dad everything. About the pet-sitting idea to adopt a chimp. About Lady Macbeth the hedgehog and Mango and Puck the gold-fish. About Rocky the parrot, who curses like a sailor.

"Grandma thought that was your friend," Dad says. "She was going to call his mother."

I tell him about Fluffernutter and Houdini and how Houdini got away.

"Oh. Oh dear." Dad presses his lips together like he's trying not to laugh.

"Why are you *laughing*?" My eyes sting with tears. "Houdini belongs to my *principal*!"

"I'm sorry," Dad says. "But do you know who Houdini was?"

"Yeah. A hamster I was in charge of and lost."

Dad smiles and sits down on my bed. "The *real* Houdini — the original Houdini — was a famous magician whose specialty was escaping from all sorts of boxes and cages. I suspect your principal chose that name because she knew her pet was a bit of an escape artist, too."

"That sure would have been a good thing for her to tell us," I say.

Dad nods. "We'll search again today. And if he doesn't turn up," Dad says, "you'll just have to tell her the truth." He picks up Bob the Lion from my bed and hands him to me.

I pull Bob close. Bob always stays where he's supposed to. "And then there's Bitsy," I say.

Dad tips his head. "And Bitsy is . . . ?"

"I thought she was going to be a hermit crab," I say. "But when she got here, she was a big python."

Dad practically chokes on his coffee. "How big?"

"About six feet."

Dad's eyes are huge. "Are you telling me there's a six-foot python in our basement right now?"

"Not exactly," I say.

"Good," Dad says.

"Because Bitsy escaped, too."

"What?" Dad puts down his coffee and jumps up, looking all around the room as if Bitsy might pop out and surprise him. "Marty, we have to call animal control. A snake that size could be —"

"Mrs. Baxter said she's gentle. She's been handled since she was a baby."

"I suppose that's good news." Dad doesn't sound convinced.

"And it doesn't matter because we've looked everywhere and she's just not here." My tears start up again.

"Let's go downstairs," Dad says.

So we do. I show Dad Lady Macbeth. She chuffs at him.

I show him the hamster cage. Houdini is still missing. Dad says hi to Fluffernutter.

I introduce him to Rocky.

"Hi there, big fella!" Dad says.

Rocky calls Dad the bad parking-lot name.

Finally, Dad turns to the giant empty snake cage, takes a deep breath, and says, "I think we need to call Mom."

"Dad, no! She only has one day left at the chimp sanctuary."

"I know, but . . ." He opens his mouth but nothing comes out for a few seconds. "I don't care how gentle Mrs. Baxter says this snake is. I am not going to catch a six-foot python. And I certainly don't know how you thought you were going to. Did you even think about it, Marty?"

"I guess not really." I don't tell him that I was imagining it kind of like playing hide-and-seek with Annie. When I find her, she always says, "Aw, you got me!" and crawls on out from the closet or wherever. Bitsy doesn't talk, of course, but I imagined her looking kind of defeated and slithering back to her cage. That sounds dumb now, even to me. "But it's Mom's last day. What if we wait until after dinner and see if we find them?"

"And if we do? If we find this big Bitsy snake, then what?"

I know Dad's right. I can't catch Bitsy and neither can he. There's only one person I know, other than Mrs. Baxter and Mom, who might be okay with scooping up a six-foot snake and hauling it back to its cage.

I take a deep breath. "Can we call Grandma Barb instead?"

chapter 15

Grandma Barb gets to our house, and she doesn't mention anything about wild hamsters or pythons running loose. When Dad called her, they decided that life would be better if Grandma Joyce didn't find out. So Dad's convinced Grandma Joyce to head home "for some peace and quiet" while Grandma Barb helps us out with dinner tonight.

"So good to see you!" Grandma Barb gives Grandma Joyce a hug.

Grandma Barb and Grandma Joyce get along, even though they're nothing alike.

Grandma Joyce reads historical novels with people kissing on the covers. She bakes tuna casserole and gives me paper dolls with frilly dresses for my birthday.

Grandma Barb reads books about building bat houses. She bakes mud pudding with gummy worms and gives me frog nets and bug catchers for my birthday.

Grandma Barb is the cool grandma. I'm really hoping she's the snake-and-hamster-catching grandma, too.

But Grandma Joyce wants to visit and have tea before she goes home, so we are sitting quietly in the living room instead of snake and hamster searching. Grandma Joyce and Dad are on the couch, and Grandma Barb and I are in the rocking chairs on the other side of the coffee table. We both like rocking better than sitting still.

Grandma Barb asks Grandma Joyce what she's been reading.

Grandma Joyce tells her about her kissy-history book.

Grandma Joyce asks Grandma Barb how her vegetable garden is doing.

Grandma Barb tells her it's good except for the cabbage worms she has to keep picking off her broccoli. "They're so tiny they're tough to get ahold of, you know?"

Grandma Joyce nods, even though she's never picked a worm off anything.

And then there's a rustle under the couch.

Grandma Joyce tips her head. "Did you hear something?"

There is another rustle. A plastic-bag-from-Shop-a-Lot kind of rustle.

"That," Grandma says. "Did you hear that?"

"Nope," I say. I did, though. It was almost as loud as my heart, which is pounding like crazy. I can't stop staring at the bottom of the couch.

"Probably just the springs on this old thing." Dad shifts his weight on the couch. It creaks a little, and then there's another rustle, and the flap of fabric that comes down from the sofa to keep you from seeing all the dust and LEGOs and stuff underneath moves a little.

"Anyway," Grandma Barb says, "aside from the cabbage worms, things are good. I'm going to have tomatoes the size of grapefruits."

"Oh, I think you're exaggerating," Grandma Joyce says, and crosses one leg neatly over the other right before a smooth, scaly head pokes out from under the sofa near her ankle.

I gasp.

"Are you all right, Marty?" Grandma Joyce says.

"Uh . . ." I make myself nod and try to keep my eyes from following Bitsy as she slithers out from under the sofa along the side where Grandma Joyce and Dad can't see.

"I . . . um . . ." I look at Grandma Barb. She can see the snake, too, I can tell, but she shakes her head at me the tiniest bit and just keeps on talking while the snake heads for the hallway.

"You know, I always end up with a bumper crop of zucchini. Do you have any recipes, Joyce?"

Grandma Joyce has recipes for everything. She tells Grandma Barb about two of her favorites for zucchini while Bitsy disappears into the bathroom off the front hallway.

Then Grandma Barb stands up and stretches. "Well, I'm sure you don't want to get too late a start driving home. I need to use the ladies' room, so I'll say good-bye now."

Grandma Barb hugs Grandma Joyce and heads for the bathroom.

She steps inside and closes the door. I stare at it and hold my breath.

"Marty? Are you forgetting your manners?" Dad says.

I turn and give Grandma Joyce a hug and kiss good-bye. "Thanks for all the cookies and everything."

"Tell Rachel I said hello," Grandma Joyce says, picking up her suitcase and heading for the door, "and remind her to clean under that kitchen sink more often. There were mouse droppings everywhere."

Just as the porch door slams shut, there's a *thump-swish-thump* from the bathroom.

"You okay in there?" Dad calls.

"Just fine," Grandma Barb says.

"The coast is clear, Grandma," I call, and Dad's mouth just about unhinges when she swings open the bathroom door and walks out with Bitsy draped around her shoulders. Grandma is holding Bitsy's neck with one hand, just behind her jaw, but Bitsy doesn't look upset to be caught. Maybe she was ready to be found after all.

chapter 16

"If we can just find Houdini now, we'll be all set." I follow Grandma Barb down to the basement.

Grandma doesn't say anything as she uncoils Bitsy's tail from her arm and lowers the snake, loop by loop, back into her cage. Bitsy stretches out as long as she can and looks happy to be home. Grandma closes the lid, checks for openings, and puts a big pile of books on top so Bitsy can't move the broken part. She stands there with her arms crossed, looking down at the snake.

"Mission accomplished!" I say. "Well, half accomplished, but a hamster ought to be a piece of cake after this, right?"

"Well . . ." Grandma sighs.

"What's wrong?" I ask. I know we still have a missing hamster, but I feel like now that we've got Bitsy back, we're kind of on a roll.

"Unfortunately," Grandma says, "I think we've found your missing hamster."

"What?" Man, is she good. She must have spotted Houdini and scooped him up without me even noticing. But then the rest of what she said sinks in. "Wait . . . why is it unfortunate? And where's Houdini?"

"Oh, Marty." She puts an arm around me, pulls me close to her, and points into Bitsy's cage. "See the lump about a third of the way down the snake's body?"

I see it. But my stomach feels so awful and twisty that I can't answer her to say yes.

"That's what a python looks like after it's . . . had a meal. I'm afraid Bitsy found Houdini before we did," Grandma says quietly.

I stare and stare at the lump. It's just a bulge in the snake's scaly body, but I imagine Houdini's fluffiness all trapped inside, and I start to cry.

Grandma doesn't say it'll be okay, because it won't be. Grandma Barb doesn't lie about stuff like that. She just rubs my back while I cry and cry and try to catch my breath.

When I do, and my eyes clear a little, that big ugly bulge is still there. For a second, I hate Bitsy for eating Houdini, but right away, I know who I should really hate is me. "I'm the worst pet-sitter ever!" I sob into Grandma's shoulder.

"No," she says. "I doubt that very much. Here's what we're going to do. We're going out right now to buy a replacement lid for Bitsy's cage. I'll pay for it and you can pay me back when you earn the money. Are all these pets getting picked up tomorrow?"

"Yes." Thinking about that makes me cry harder.

"Marty." Grandma pulls me into a hug. "You didn't do any of this on purpose. Everybody makes mistakes, and —"

"Not mistakes that end with one of the pets you're sitting eating another one."

Grandma sighs. "That's true. And Mrs. Grimes is going to be sad when you tell her what happened. But she knows that you're a good, kind girl who loves animals."

I picture myself telling Mrs. Grimes what happened. My stomach hurts. "Will you be here tomorrow?" I ask Grandma.

She nods. "Yes, I will. Your dad is going to pick up your mom, but I'll be here."

"Will you tell Mrs. Grimes what happened?"

"No. You need to do that. But I'll be right beside you, I promise." Grandma hugs me again and heads upstairs.

I look over at poor lonely Fluffernutter in the cage and think about telling Mrs. Grimes she only has one sad hamster now.

Tomorrow is going to be the worst day of my life.

chapter 17

"I still can't believe she ate Houdini." Rupert stares into the snake cage.

"What time is Mrs. Grimes coming?" Rasheena asks.

"Around three." I turn to Annie. "Thanks for calling everybody when Grandma told you what happened."

"We were all pet-sitting," she says, "so it's really all of our responsibility to be here today."

Even Alex came over, but he's staying far away from Bitsy. "Has the hedgehog gotten any friend-lier?" He reaches down to pet her, but she chuffs so loud he yanks his hand back. "Guess not."

"She should have given Houdini a lesson in how not to get eaten," Rupert says. "Be prickly and make scary noises."

"That's not funny," I say. Poor Houdini was the cutest, fluffiest thing ever and didn't

deserve to get eaten. "I wish we'd fed Bitsy that frozen mouse earlier."

Annie comes to stand next to me. "Mrs. Baxter said to feed Bitsy on Saturday. You were following directions."

The doorbell rings, and a minute later, Grandma Barb calls down, "Marty, your librarian is here!"

We come up with the hedgehog cage and fishbowl, and Ms. Stephanie rushes to Lady Macbeth and scoops her up out of the cage. Lady Macbeth doesn't make a single chuff. "Hello, my girl!" Ms. Stephanie smiles at me. "Thank you so much, Marty. I know this is going

to a great cause." She hands me twenty-five dollars. I can't bring myself to tell her that it's going to pay for the cage I broke instead of bananas and toys for chimps.

Mr. Klein arrives after lunch.

Grandma Barb helps me bring the parrot cage upstairs. "He has a rather colorful vocabulary," she says, handing the cage to Mr. Klein out on the porch.

"Err . . . yes. We're working on that." Mr. Klein hands me fifteen dollars. "Thanks a lot, kids!" He heads for his truck with Rocky just as Mrs. Baxter pulls up in her car.

"Well, hello again, birdie!" she coos at Rocky as Mr. Klein passes her on the sidewalk.

"Hello! Stupid jerk!"

Mr. Klein loads Rocky into his backseat and speeds away.

"So how did it go?" Mrs. Baxter says as she climbs the porch steps. Grandma Barb holds the kitchen door open for her and raises her eyebrows at me, waiting for me to answer.

I swallow a lump in my throat. "Not good," I say.

Mrs. Baxter's eyes get all wide and worried until Grandma Barb says, "Bitsy is fine. I'll let Marty explain the rest while I go get her. Do you kids want to help me?"

"Sure!" Rasheena says. "Come on, Alex."

Alex's face turns a little pale, but he follows them downstairs. Annie and Rupert stay with me.

"Mrs. Baxter," Annie begins, "Bitsy is okay, but we did have a problem that we need to tell you about."

I take a deep breath. "Bitsy didn't eat the frozen mouse you left us."

"That's okay," Mrs. Baxter says.

"She ate a hamster instead," Rupert says.

"Oh." Mrs. Baxter presses her lips together. "That's not okay. Was it . . . someone's pet?"

I nod. "Mrs. Grimes."

"Oh." She frowns. "How did the hamster get into Bitsy's cage?"

"It didn't. Bitsy got out. Actually, the hamster got out first, and then we were looking for Bitsy and the hamster, but Bitsy found the hamster before we found Bitsy."

"Oh. Well . . ." She fumbles in her purse. "Here's the money I owe for pet-sitting. I'm so sorry about the hamster."

"You shouldn't feel bad. It's not your fault. Or Bitsy's," I add. "It's mine."

Grandma and Rasheena and Alex bring the cage up to the kitchen, and I remember I messed that up, too. "I knocked off the top of her cage, too. We bought a new one and put it on, so that should be okay now." I hand back the money. "I can't take this from you when I did such a crummy job."

She pushes the wad of bills back to me. "It's for the chimps," she says, and pats me on the shoulder. Then she eyes the bulge in Bitsy's middle. "Has Mrs. Grimes come to pick up her hamsters — err — her hamster yet?"

I shake my head. "She should be here soon."

"Oh dear." She crouches down and looks me right in the eyes. "I'm sure this won't be easy, Marty, but Mrs. Grimes knows you're a good kid. Everybody makes mistakes sometimes." That makes me feel a little better. But I notice that Mrs. Baxter isn't in any hurry to see Mrs. Grimes. She grabs one end of Bitsy's cage, and Grandma Barb gets the other, and they take Bitsy to the car to go home.

It's a whole awful half hour before Mrs. Grimes rings the doorbell. We've been waiting with poor Fluffernutter in her cage on the kitchen table, and when I open the door for Mrs. Grimes, she rushes right over.

"Hello, my precious little girl!" She scoops Fluffernutter up and kisses her and then looks back down at the cage. "Where's Houdini?"

I open my mouth but nothing comes out.

Annie rescues me. "Mrs. Grimes," she says. "We are so, so sorry, but when I was feeding Fluffernutter and Houdini on Friday morning, I must not have put the lid on right."

"We didn't notice, so we went to school, and when we got home, he was gone," I say. All I can see in my head is the lump in Bitsy's middle, and the lump in my throat keeps getting bigger and bigger. "We looked everywhere, but —"

"Oh, that Houdini," Mrs. Grimes says, laughing. "He'll turn up when you least expect it. He breaks out of that cage at least once a week. I should have warned you. That's where his name comes from. Do you know about the other Houdini?"

"My dad told me, but Mrs. Grimes, listen." I blurt it out. "He's not going to turn up this time. I'm so, so sorry, but we were also pet-sitting Mrs. Baxter's —"

"Marty Elizabeth McGuire!" Grandma Joyce comes bursting in from the porch holding a shoe box way out in front of her. "Can you explain what this was doing in my suitcase?"

"I didn't put anything in there!" I did put a frog in Grandma Joyce's suitcase once when she came to visit, but I was way younger then and I promised Dad I'd never do it again because Grandma Joyce doesn't think things like that are funny.

"I suppose it crawled in all by itself?" She shoves the box toward me, and when I lift the lid, there's a fluffy yellow face poking up at me.

"Houdini!"

"Really?" Annie squeals.

Rasheena rushes over to the box, too. "It's really him!"

It is. And I feel like I just got my whole life back.

"See!" Mrs. Grimes claps her hands. "He always turns up, the little rascal."

"Turns up?" Grandma Joyce harrumphs. "That rodent jumped out of my suitcase when I opened it up. Almost gave me a heart attack!"

"Wow! We totally thought he got eaten!" Rupert says.

"You thought *what*?" Mrs. Grimes carefully latches the lid of the hamster cage and looks up at us.

I take a deep breath. "We were also pet-sitting Mrs. Baxter's Burmese python. Bitsy got out of her cage the same day Houdini escaped, and then when we found Bitsy, she had this hamster-shaped lump in her belly, and so we just thought . . ."

"You thought the lump was Houdini." Mrs. Grimes looks down at the hamster cage. "Well, I'm certainly glad it wasn't." She pulls two neatly folded bills from her purse — a ten and a five — and hands them to me.

"I can't take this," I say, "since he got away and everything."

Mrs. Grimes shakes her head. "Take it. I should have warned you about Houdini's particular talent." She picks up the cage and heads for the door. "See you on Monday. Big talent show day!"

When she's gone, Rupert and Rasheena and Alex head home for dinner. Annie and I sit on the porch.

"Want to stay for dinner?" I ask.

"I can't," she says. "I'm practicing for the talent show with Veronica Grace and Isabel. You can still do cartwheels with us, you know."

"No, that's okay," I say. "My mom's coming home soon and I want to see her. Besides, you guys have practiced a ton. I don't want to mess it up like I did the pet-sitting."

"We still raised money to adopt a chimp, didn't we?"

I shake my head and tell her about the new lid we had to buy for the snake cage. "It took all the pet-sitting money and I still owe Grandma Barb three dollars when I get my allowance."

"Well," she says. "There's always the talent show. See you tomorrow!"

I go inside and give Grandma Barb the money I owe her. "Well," she says, tucking it in her pocket. "I guess things worked out all right in the end."

"Not really," I say. "All our money from the fund-raiser ended up paying for food and the broken lid and stuff. We didn't raise anything for the chimps."

Grandma nods. "Some fund-raisers are more successful than others." Then she pulls a twenty-dollar bill back out of her pocket. "Here's a donation for your next round. I'm sure you can come up with another great idea, and you'll be adopting your chimp in no time."

"Thanks." I take the money and think about that. But the truth is . . . after this pet-sitting mess, I'm a little afraid of having any more great ideas right now.

In a little while, Dad gets home with Mom, and I give her the biggest hug ever. I'm so happy she's home, even though I'm probably in trouble with her now, too.

Grandma Joyce starts to poke around in the refrigerator for tuna casserole ingredients, but Grandma Barb offers to order Tony's pizza instead, and even Grandma Joyce thinks that's a good idea.

Mom tells us all about working with the chimps. They're amazing and smart, and it's heartbreaking what they've all been through, she says. It makes me even sadder that I messed up our chance to raise money for them. But I love seeing all her pictures of the chimps grooming one another and playing with kid toys and even putting on people clothes. One loves to wear hats and has a whole collection of them. Mom puts all the pictures on a digital storage thing so I can take them to school tomorrow to show Annie on the classroom computer.

I tell Mom all about our pet-sitting mess, about my hedgehog bite and the escapees, and about Rocky who curses like a sailor. Mom shakes her head and keeps looking at Dad. I think he's in trouble, too.

"Here's what I don't understand," Mom says, frowning. "If Houdini stowed away in Grandma Joyce's suitcase, what was that bulge in the snake?"

"I don't know. She must have found something else to eat."

Dad shrugs. "I can't imagine what."

"Are you kidding?" Grandma Joyce says. She stands up, walks over to the cupboard under the sink, and flings open the door. "I told you that you have mice."

We're cleaning up from dinner when the doorbell rings. I answer it, and it's a man I don't

recognize. But then I look down and see Sarah from the playground.

"Hi!" she says. "I'm here for Joyce."

"I'm Joyce," Grandma steps up to the door and smiles. "What's your name?"

Sarah frowns. "You're not Joyce."

"Well, yes," Grandma says, "I am."

Sarah shakes her head. "Joyce is a slug."

"Oh . . ." Grandma says.

"Her house is ready," Sarah explains, and holds up a red clay dish thing with a wobbly lid.

"It's very nice," I say. "Be right back." I go downstairs, get the coffee mug full of lettuce and Joyce the Slug, and hand it to Sarah. She dumps the lettuce and slug into Joyce's new house and then holds the slimy coffee mug out to Grandma. "Is this yours, Other Joyce?"

"Thank you." Grandma takes the mug and looks at me while Sarah skips back to the car. "Marty, are there any more pets we should know about?"

"Nope. Joyce was the last of the bunch," I tell her. "I promise."

chapter 18

I want to go to the library to return my pet-care books Monday morning. But I can't even ask Mrs. Aloi because everybody's busy practicing for the talent show.

Annie and Veronica Grace and Isabel are dancing in the hallway.

Mr. Farley is here with the real saw today — no more imaginary tools for Alex.

Kimmy came to school in a tall, poofy chef's hat. She brought all her cupcake ingredients and measuring cups and mixing bowls, and it looks like she's been practicing a lot because she has chocolate cupcake batter all over her face.

Emma is playing "Happy Birthday" on her recorder. Jimmy keeps trying to burp along with her.

"Quit it!" she says. "This is not supposed to be a duet!"

Rasheena's wearing her hockey uniform, and she's got a hockey stick and a big bucket of tennis balls that she's spilled onto the floor. She's whacking them, one by one, at Rupert, who's on the other side of the classroom padded up with goalie gear. One of the balls goes flying out the door.

"Hey!" someone shouts from the hallway.

"Sorry!" Mrs. Aloi hollers, and then gives her maracas a shake. "Listen up, everyone! We need to bring the volume level down. And, Jimmy, did I hear you burping a minute ago?"

"Yes," Emma tattles. "He was burping along with my song and he wouldn't stop."

"Sorry, Mrs. Aloi." Jimmy puts both hands up in the air in defeat. "I promise you will never hear me burp the 'Happy Birthday' song again."

"Good," she says, and rushes over to Alex and his dad to figure out where they can keep the saw until the show.

"I'm doing the ABC song for the show," Jimmy whispers to Rupert. "And then if people won't stop clapping, I'm going to burp 'Row, Row, Row Your Boat' as my encore."

Finally, Mrs. Aloi wanders over to my desk. "Marty, what did you decide to do for the show?"

"Nothing," I say. "May I please go to the library?"

Mrs. Aloi pulls up a chair. That means I am not going to the library any time soon. "What happened?" she asks.

"Nothing. I just don't have any talent," I say. "Can I go to the library now?"

"I hear you had some pet-sitting troubles," she says.

Oh. That. "You heard?"

Mrs. Aloi nods. "Mrs. Baxter said her snake ate Mrs. Grimes's hamster."

"Actually, no. We thought she ate Houdini but really Houdini went home with my grandmother in her suitcase and turned up later." I should tell Mrs. Baxter that. She'll probably be really happy to know that lump in her snake is just some mouse and not the principal's pet.

"Well, that's good news," Mrs. Aloi says. She ducks to avoid one of Rasheena's hockey-swatted tennis balls. "Careful!" she calls, and then turns back to me. "So why aren't you doing the talent show?"

"Because I was supposed to do a thing with Annie and Veronica Grace and Isabel, only I got too busy with the pet-sitting and never practiced. I didn't want to do cartwheels anyway. I just wanted to help the chimps."

"Well, that's great," Mrs. Aloi says. "How much money did you raise pet-sitting?"

"Negative three dollars," I tell her, and explain about the ruined snake cage. "I just wanted to help. I mean, my mom spent a whole week at the sanctuary, and the chimps are amazing. Do you know how smart they are? They play with people toys and eat regular salads and drink smoothies and stuff, just like we do. And they all have best friends, Mom says. Like this one chimp, Rosco, hangs out with one named Chloe all the time. Just like Annie and me."

Mrs. Aloi smiles. "They sound incredible."

"They are," I say. And I remember the pictures Mom gave me to show Annie. "You can see them if you want."

I load up the photos on the classroom computer, and I tell Mrs. Aloi all Mom's stories from the sanctuary. Funny stories, like how the chimp named Skipper loves to play practical jokes, and cute stories, like how the one named Mac wears fancy ladies' hats and carries around a doll like it's his baby. And sad stories, too, like about old Joe, who spent almost all his life in a tiny cage in a research lab and only got to live at the sanctuary a couple years before he died.

"That's the only reason I wanted to do the talent show," I tell her after she's seen the last photo. It's a picture of Carol the sanctuary lady holding one of the chimps' hands. Their fingers look so much alike. "I wanted to help them. Only I don't have a talent."

Mrs. Aloi looks at the picture on the screen. Then she looks at me. "You're wrong, Marty. You do have a talent. And I know just what it is."

chapter 19

When we get to the auditorium, the first and second graders are in their seats ready to watch. We file in behind them to wait for our turn to be onstage.

"Everybody ready?" Mrs. Aloi whispers down the row.

What I'm about to do is way scarier than turning a few cartwheels, but I find Grandma Barb in the crowd and she waves at me and that makes me feel better.

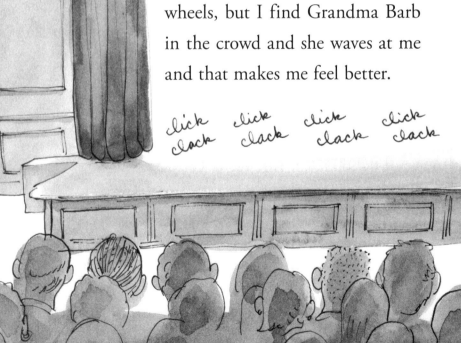

click click click click
clack clack clack clack

Mom and Dad are there and Grandma Joyce, too. She holds up a bag of cookies she's got all packed up for me and smiles.

Mrs. Grimes comes down the hall, gives us a finger-to-her-lips *shhhh*, and hurries past us onto the wooden stage, where her shoes are especially clickety-clackety. Walking in those high heels is her special talent.

"Good morning, students, staff, families, and guests," Mrs. Grimes says.

ick
clack

"Our third graders have been practicing for this show all week. And let me tell you, they are one talented group."

The audience claps.

"As you may have seen on the posters on your way in," Mrs. Grimes says, "our students are requesting donations for a chimpanzee sanctuary. Although we don't charge admission for today's show, they would love if you'd support their efforts." She looks down at her talent list. "Our first talent today will be performed by Kimmy Butler."

Kimmy goes up in her chef's hat, and Mrs. Baxter wheels a cafeteria cart onto the stage with all her cooking stuff.

"Hi there!" Kimmy says into the microphone. It makes her voice sound super loud. I bet people would be impressed if she didn't still have chocolate all over her face. "Today we're going to make chocolate–chocolate chip cupcakes with chocolate frosting and chocolate sprinkles. First, you need cupcake mix and oil and eggs."

She's got that stuff measured out, so she just dumps it all into the big mixing bowl. "Then you mix it up really good."

Kimmy mixes with so much enthusiasm little clouds of chocolate fly up out of the bowl. "And then you pour cupcake batter into little cups and put it in the oven." She looks around for the little cups. But apparently, she forgot those, so she just stands there.

Finally, she decides to improvise. That's something we learned from the college theater teacher who came to help us with our class play a while ago. Improvising means you wing it. And that's what Kimmy does.

"If you find that you're missing your cupcake pan," she says, "the batter is also delicious eaten with a spoon." And she takes a big mouthful.

Everybody claps, and Mrs. Baxter helps Kimmy wheel the cupcake stuff offstage.

Isabel, Annie, and Veronica Grace go next. Their dance thing — okay, dance *extravaganza* — is actually not bad. You can tell they practiced a ton because they all spin and kick and do everything at exactly the same time except once when Isabel forgets to stop twirling. The routine is active and fast, and I like the beat.

Alex brings his saw and boards and stuff onstage next for his demonstration. Sawing takes a really, really long time, it turns out.

"I realize I'm going over the three-minute time limit," Alex says after about five minutes are up. He's a little out of breath. "But rushing is the number one mistake that craftsmen make and the number one cause of accidents." He stops sawing altogether, holds a finger up in the air, and says, "Safety first!" Then he goes back to sawing. When the board finally splits into two pieces a few minutes later, everybody claps like crazy, and Alex takes a huge bow.

Then Emma plays her recorder.

"Whose birthday is it?" some-
one calls out when she finishes.

"Nobody's! It doesn't have to be somebody's birthday to play that song, you know." And she huffs offstage. She reminds me of Lady Macbeth.

Rasheena and Rupert are next with their hockey skit,

which is really just Rasheena whipping tennis balls at Rupert and Rupert diving across the floor trying to stop them. Mostly, he doesn't, but he looks cool flopping all over in that big goalie outfit.

Jimmy burps his ABCs next, and Mrs. Aloi looks so mad that I think she might run up there and drag him offstage the way they do on cartoons when somebody's singing badly. But she doesn't. And when he finishes, the audience claps so loud that he burps "Row, Row, Row Your Boat," too.

Then it's my turn. My stomach is kind of twisty feeling when I go up onstage. There's no music or anything. Just me talking, and on the big screen behind me, the photographs from the sanctuary that Ms. Stephanie helped me put into a slideshow.

"I'd like to introduce you to some amazing relatives of ours," I say as the first picture comes up on the screen. "This is Rosco." He's drinking a smoothie out of a cup just the way a person would, and that makes everyone in the audience say, "Awww."

"Rosco is a chimpanzee," I say. "Chimpanzees are supposed to live in the rain forests of Africa with their families. They live in big groups of up to a few dozen chimps. Imagine that if you think your family is big!"

That gets a laugh from the audience and makes me feel pretty good.

"But Rosco never lived in Africa. Neither did Joe or Skipper or Chloe or Mac." I click the remote Ms. Stephanie gave me to show pictures of the other chimps, and then I click again so the screen changes to a photo from one of those research labs. "These chimps spent almost their whole lives in cages because they were used in scientific research projects." I can feel my voice getting louder because I think that's just so wrong, but Ms. Stephanie told me I had to be fair and give both sides of the issue so that people would know I did my research. So I go on.

"Some people argue that's okay because the research might help cure diseases in humans. But I disagree because we know so much about chimps now — how they communicate and solve problems and play." The photo changes to a picture of Rosco in a funny cowboy hat. "We know they care for one another and make friends and laugh. Just like us."

Then I tell the hard part. "These chimps were kept in tiny cages for years, and many of them were injected with germs that made them sick. They'll never be able to live in the wild. But at this sanctuary, there's a chimp house and a playground and gardens." I click through the slides. "And people to take care of them and make sure their last years on Earth are better than the ones that came before. Carol — she runs the sanctuary — figures we owe the chimps that much." I click to

the last slide, a close-up of a chimp's face with big, warm eyes. "And I think so, too."

People start clapping before I'm done. "Hey, wait! I didn't tell you what to do yet!" Ms. Stephanie holds up a finger for me to wait. When they stop clapping, I say, "Please donate some money to help us adopt a chimp if you can. That doesn't mean you get to take it home," I say, just in case anybody's getting excited. "It means our money will help care for that chimp, and we'll get updates on how it's doing and stuff. Okay?"

They clap again and finally, I get to go sit down, and Mrs. Grimes thanks everybody for coming, and it's all done.

Grandma Barb finds me right away. "That was spectacular!" she says, and kisses the top of my head.

"Outstanding," Mom says. She and Dad thank

Ms. Stephanie for helping me with my presentation while everybody's leaving.

"Were you nervous?" Grandma Joyce asks, handing me her bag of cookies.

"Kind of," I say. "But I had to do it, you know? It was for a good cause, even though it'll probably be forever before we can adopt a chimp now."

Ms. Stephanie packs up the computer and projector, and we all help Mr. Klein put away the extra chairs.

"Marty, look!" Annie comes rushing up to us with our adopt-a-chimp jar, which is full — and I mean dollars-spilling-out-the-top full — of money. "People loved your talk! With this and the money Grandma Barb donated, we're going to have enough to adopt at least three chimps! Maybe four!"

"Oh, wow!" I say.

"Fantastic news!" Mr. Klein says. "But does

this mean you're not going to do any more pet-sitting?"

"Yes," Dad says at the same time Annie and I say, "No."

"Because I'm going to be visiting my brother out west soon," Mr. Klein says. "Any chance you'd like to take care of Rocky again?"

"I'd love to!" I say. But then I look up at Mom and Dad. "Can I? Please?"

Grandma Joyce harrumphs. "That bird should have its mouth washed out with soap," she says.

Mr. Klein laughs. "I've been working with him on that. 'Mind your manners, dumb bird,' is one of his favorite new sayings."

"That's an improvement," Dad says. "It's okay with me if Rocky visits again."

"But listen, Marty," Mom says. "Any animal-care business you set up in the future is going to be a one-pet-at-a-time operation. Understood?"

"Understood." One pet at a time — plus a few adopted chimpanzees — sounds just right.

author's note

Great Ape Sanctuary, the chimpanzee sanctuary Marty visits in this book, is fictional, but it is modeled after the real primate rescue centers that are part of the North American Primate Sanctuary Alliance.

That organization was founded in 2010 "to advance the welfare of captive primates through exceptional sanctuary care, collaboration, and outreach." Simply put, it's an organization designed to provide chimps with safe, comfortable places to live when they can't be released into the wild.

As of June 2013, there are eight chimp sanctuaries in North America, located in Florida, Kentucky, Louisiana, Ohio, Oregon, Quebec, and Washington State. All of them rely on the generosity and creativity of people like Marty to help take care of the chimps. If you'd like to work with your family or classroom to adopt a chimp (remember, you don't actually get to take it home!) or donate in another way, visit the North American Primate Sanctuary Alliance online: www.primatesanctuaries.org.

At the website, you can read about all the different sanctuaries and visit their websites. Each one has information on the chimps who live there and how you can help.